School Stars
Times Tables

Scholastic Children's Books,
Euston House, 24 Eversholt Street,
London NW1 1DB, UK

A division of Scholastic Ltd
London ~ New York ~ Toronto ~ Sydney ~ Auckland
Mexico City ~ New Delhi ~ Hong Kong

Published in the UK by Scholastic Ltd, 2015

Text by Chris Baker
Illustrations by Lee Robinson
© Scholastic Children's Books, 2015

ISBN 978 1407 15814 3

Printed and bound by Thumprints, Malaysia

2 4 6 8 10 9 7 5 3 1

scholastic.co.uk

Guide for Parents

This book will help your child learn and practise the times tables that are usually taught in schools in Year 2 and Year 3. (Usually the two, ten and five times tables are taught in Year 2, and the three, four and eight times tables in Year 3.)

Each table is introduced and your child is invited to memorize it. We point out one of the patterns in the table and also revise basic facts about multiplication. Then there are some fun activities and games your child can use to practise.

The book also comes with game cards. These can be used as flash cards, or to practise tables by playing games such as Matches, Dominoes or Find Your Alien Name. You'll find all the instructions about how to play on pages 30, 31 and 32.

The ideal is for children to learn to recall the times table calculations quickly and without effort, and to be able to use that knowledge flexibly. Memorizing the tables – if your child can – is a good approach. Please remember though that some children find it very easy to memorize information: others find it much more difficult, and this isn't necessarily to do with intelligence. It is really important to work at a speed that is right for your child. In particular, try to avoid a 'cycle of failure', when your child cannot remember the answer and becomes anxious, frustrated or ashamed. Sometimes this cycle starts because parents or carers demand quick answers before their child is secure at answering at all.

You can help your child by:

⭐ Providing a good environment in which to work, with few distractions.

⭐ Stopping if your child is unproductively tired or frustrated (memorizing can be hard work: work in short bursts; do more later).

⭐ Switching between activities often: rote-learning, activities, flash cards and games.

⭐ Noticing what works for your child and doing more of that. Some will like rote memorization, others will prefer the games.

⭐ Using tables with your child in real-life situations:
• for calculations: for example, "How many eggs are in this box" or "How many floor tiles are in this room?"
• in games: if you're learning the two times table on a journey, for example, you could award two points for each time your child spots a silver car. This will get your child either counting in twos, or keeping a count of objects and then doing a tables calculations later to get the score.

⭐ Praise effort as well as results – this can be crucial to encourage children who are slightly slower at memorizing.

The Two Times Table

Read the two times table. Then close the book
and write it out – how much can you remember?

✓1 x 2 = 2	✓5 x 2 = 10	✓9 x 2 = 18
✓2 x 2 = 4	✓6 x 2 = 12	✓10 x 2 = 20
✓3 x 2 = 6	✓7 x 2 = 14	✓11 x 2 = 22
✓4 x 2 = 8	✓8 x 2 = 16	12 x 2 = 24

Practise the two times table until you know it, then you can move on
to the games! You can also use the flash cards in the middle of the
book to help – turn to page 30 to find out how.

Fill in the answers below. Make sure you cover up the
answers above first.

10 __ x 2 = 20   8 x __ = 16   _8_ = 4 x 2

5 x __ = 10   6 x 2 = _12_   11 x _2_ = 22

3 x 2 = __   __ x 2 = 24   2 x 2 = __

__ = 7 x 2   __ = 1 x 2   __ x 2 = 18

Good Job!

Good

Patterns

All the answers in the two times table end in 2, 4, 6, 8 or 0. Any of these numbers can be divided exactly by 2. We call these numbers 'even'.

$1 \times 2 = 2$ $5 \times 2 = 10$ $9 \times 2 = 18$

$2 \times 2 = 4$ $6 \times 2 = 12$ $10 \times 2 = 20$

$3 \times 2 = 6$ $7 \times 2 = 14$ $11 \times 2 = 22$

$4 \times 2 = 8$ $8 \times 2 = 16$ $12 \times 2 = 24$

Number Square Colouring

★ ★ ★
STAR TIP!
We can write the answer before or after the sum:
$5 \times 2 = 10$
$10 = 5 \times 2$
★ ★ ★

1	2	3	4	5
6	7	8	9	10
11	12	13	14	15
16	17	18	19	20
21	22	23	24	25

Colour all the numbers that are answers in the two times table.

Mystery Picture

Colour in all the squares that have answers in the two times table. What picture do you get?

13	67	14	65	75	91	79	10	29	55
99	49	23	4	35	63	24	77	31	23
75	33	19	45	18	2	17	23	95	71
41	22	16	10	12	8	22	14	8	95
20	2	18	12	24	12	2	10	24	2
12	14	10	●	8	4	●	20	12	18
6	24	4	12	10	22	6	14	12	4
85	10	2	⋁⋁⋁⋁				18	20	35
45	33	18	24	16	14	2	12	33	79
83	55	37	71	43	69	25	97	51	13

Maths Machine

This machine multiplies any number put into it by 2. Fill in the missing numbers.

2 →
→
7 →
9 →
→

→
→ 6
→
→
→ 22

You're a Star!

Planet Hop

Draw a safe path for the rocket. It can only travel to planets that are answers in the two times table.

22

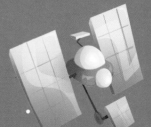
11

9

19

16

5

Home

3

21

8

13

2

Crack the Door Code!

To open the spaceship door you need to enter a number code. The correct code numbers have been multiplied by 2. Find the code – the first number has been done for you:

24 = 2 × __12__

6 = 2 × ___

8 = 2 × ___

10 = 2 × ___

24   6   10
          8

The Ten Times Table

Read the ten times table. Then close the book
and write it out – how much can you remember?

1 x 10 = 10	5 x 10 = 50	9 x 10 = 90
2 x 10 = 20	6 x 10 = 60	10 x 10 = 100
3 x 10 = 30	7 x 10 = 70	11 x 10 = 110
4 x 10 = 40	8 x 10 = 80	12 x 10 = 120

Practise the ten times table until you know it, then you can
move on to the games! As before, you can also use the
flash cards in the middle of the book to help.

**Fill in the answers below. Make sure you cover up the
answers above first.**

___ x 2 = 20   12 x ___ = 120   ___ = 7 x 10

5 x ___ = 50   8 x 10 = ___   10 x ___ = 30

10 x 6 = ___   ___ x 1 = 10   11 x 10 = ___

___ = 10 x 10   ___ = 4 x 10   ___ x 9 = 90

Patterns

All the answers in the ten times table end in 0.

1 x 10 = **10**	5 x 10 = **50**	9 x 10 = **90**
2 x 10 = **20**	6 x 10 = **60**	10 x 10 = **100**
3 x 10 = **30**	7 x 10 = **70**	11 x 10 = **110**
4 x 10 = **40**	8 x 10 = **80**	12 x 10 = **120**

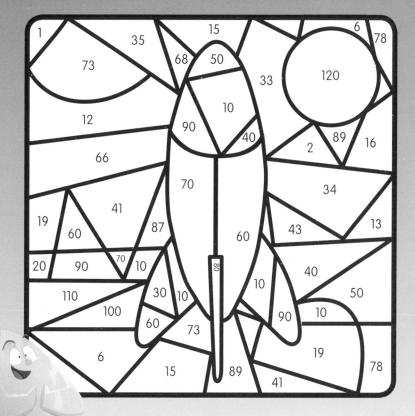

Mystery Picture

Colour in all the squares that have answers in the ten times table. What picture do you get?

9

Through the Stars

Do the tables calculations below to work out the right path to guide the rocket through the stars. Then draw a line to show the route the rocket will take.

① 12 x 10   ② 10 x 6   ③ 10 x 10   ④ 4 x 10   ⑤ 10 x 8
⑥ 1 x 10   ⑦ 9 x 10   ⑧ 3 x 10   ⑨ 2 x 10   ⑩ 7 x 10

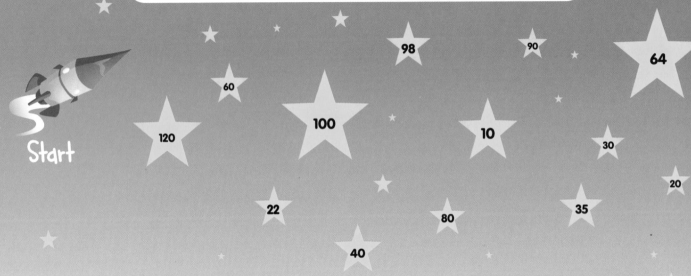

Start

98   90   64
60
120   100   10   30
                20
22   80   35
40
                70
Finish

Maths Machine

This machine multiplies any number put into it by 10. Fill in the missing numbers.

1 →   → ☐
6 →   → ☐
☐ →   x10 → 50
9 →   → ☐
11 →   → ☐

Crack the Door Code!

To open the spaceship door you need to enter a number code. The correct code numbers have been multiplied by 10. Find the code – the first number has been done for you:

$80 = 10 \times \underline{\ 8\ }$

$20 = 10 \times \underline{\hspace{1cm}}$

$90 = 10 \times \underline{\hspace{1cm}}$

$10 = 10 \times \underline{\hspace{1cm}}$

80   20   10   90

Pick Your Spaceship Crew

Draw a circle around crew members whose numbers are answers in the ten times table. How many crew members is that?

20   65   110   60   18   90   34   30

11

The Five Times Table

Read the five times table. Then close the book
and write it out – how much can you remember?

1 x 5 = 5	5 x 5 = 25	9 x 5 = 45
2 x 5 = 10	6 x 5 = 30	10 x 5 = 50
3 x 5 = 15	7 x 5 = 35	11 x 5 = 55
4 x 5 = 20	8 x 5 = 40	12 x 5 = 60

Practise the five times table until you know it. As before, you can use the flash cards in the middle of the book to help. You can now also use the cards in the book to play Matches and Dominoes too! Turn to pages 30, 31 and 32 to find out how.

Fill in the answers below. Make sure you cover up the answers above first.

___ x 2 = 10   12 x ___ = 60   ___ = 9 x 5

5 x ___ = 25   7 x 5 = ___   6 x ___ = 30

11 x 5 = ___   ___ x 1 = 5   5 x 10 = ___

___ = 8 x 5   ___ = 4 x 5   ___ x 3 = 15

Patterns

All the answers in the five times table end in 5 or 0.

1 x 5 = 5	5 x 5 = 25	9 x 5 = 45
2 x 5 = 10	6 x 5 = 30	10 x 5 = 50
3 x 5 = 15	7 x 5 = 35	11 x 5 = 55
4 x 5 = 20	8 x 5 = 40	12 x 5 = 60

Hopscotch

Write the answers from the five times table into this hopscotch court (the first few are done for you.) Now colour in the answers that also appear in the ten times table. What do you notice?

★★★ STAR TIP!
Did you notice that multiplying something by one does not change it?
1 x 5 = 5
★★★

5 | 10 | 15

Crack the Door Code!

To open the spaceship door you need to enter a number code. The correct code numbers have been multiplied by 5. Find the code – the first number has been done for you:

15 = 5 × __3__

30 = 5 × ___

60 = 5 × ___

45 = 5 × ___

22	58	89	2	18	66	11	36	91	71
48	99	11	24	53	4	32	82	46	69
91	20	2	39	25	66	40	25	5	9
69	45	58	13	5	27	52	60	63	49
13	10	98	49	55	2	77	35	1	14
77	50	10	25	30	13	6	25	26	37
16	60	53	3	45	17	69	10	71	98
54	55	12	78	15	33	5	15	30	24
82	3	44	61	73	91	36	48	16	17
33	18	7	1	28	89	47	77	8	66

Secret Message

Colour in all the squares that have answers in the five times table. What message do you get?

Red Leader

Circle the rockets that belong with Squadron Leader 20.
If they belong, their calculations have the answer 20.

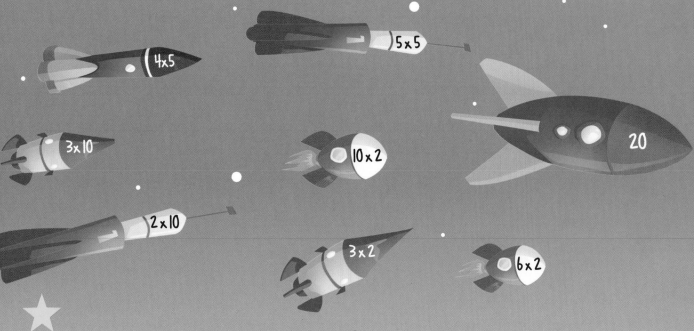

Through the Stars

Do the tables calculations below to work out the right path to guide
the rocket through the stars. Then draw a line to show the route the
rocket will take.

❶ 3 x 5   ❷ 10 x 5   ❸ 9 x 5   ❹ 1 x 5
❺ 7 x 5   ❻ 5 x 5   ❼ 6 x 5   ❽ 11 x 5

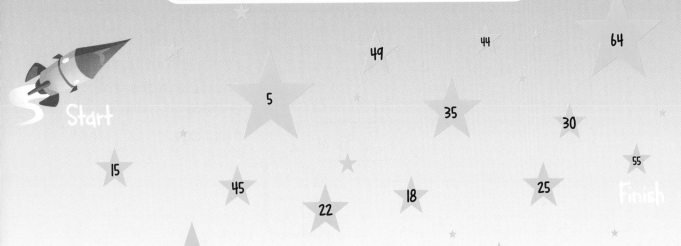

44   64

49

5   35

30

Start

55

15

45   18   25

Finish

22

50   84

The Three Times Table

Read the three times table. Then close the book
and write it out – how much can you remember?

1 x 3 = 3	5 x 3 = 15	9 x 3 = 27
2 x 3 = 6	6 x 3 = 18	10 x 3 = 30
3 x 3 = 9	7 x 3 = 21	11 x 3 = 33
4 x 3 = 12	8 x 3 = 24	12 x 3 = 36

Practise the three times table until you know it. You can use
the cards in the middle of the book as flash cards and to play
Matches and Dominoes too!

Fill in the answers below. Make sure you cover up the
answers above first.

___ x 3 = 18   12 x ___ = 36   ___ = 8 x 3

3 x ___ = 9   9 x 3 = ___   7 x ___ = 21

11 x 3 = ___   ___ x 3 = 12   3 x 2 = ___

___ = 1 x 3   ___ = 3 x 10   ___ x 3 = 15

Patterns

The digits in the answer to a three times table sum always add up to 3, 6 or 9. Any number whose digits do that must be something you can divide by 3.

$1 \times 3 = 3$

$2 \times 3 = 6$

$3 \times 3 = 9$

$4 \times 3 = 12 \; (1 + 2 = 3)$

$5 \times 3 = 15 \; (1 + 5 = 6)$

$6 \times 3 = 18 \; (1 + 8 = 9)$

$7 \times 3 = 21 \; (2 + 1 = 3)$

$8 \times 3 = 24 \; (2 + 4 = 6)$

$9 \times 3 = 27 \; (2 + 7 = 9)$

$10 \times 3 = 30 \; (3 + 0 = 3)$

$11 \times 3 = 33 \; (3 + 3 = 6)$

$12 \times 3 = 36 \; (3 + 6 = 9)$

Number Square Colouring

1	2	3	4	5	6
7	8	9	10	11	12
13	14	15	16	17	18
19	20	21	22	23	24
25	26	27	28	29	30
31	32	33	34	35	36

Colour all the numbers that are answers in the three times table.

STAR TIP!
If you multiply a number by three, you can say you are tripling it.

Maths Machine

This machine multiplies any number put into it by 3. Fill in the missing numbers.

9 →
→
2 →
→
12 →

×3

→ [ ]
→ 12
→ [ ]
→ 21
→ [ ]

Mystery Picture

Colour in all the spaces that have answers in the three times table. What picture do you get?

Pick Your Spaceship Crew

Draw a circle around crew members whose numbers are answers in the three times table. How many crew members is that?

Crack the Door Code!

To open the spaceship door you need to enter a number code. The correct code numbers have been multiplied by 3. Find the code – the first number has been done for you:

$36 = 3 \times \underline{12}$

$30 = 3 \times \underline{}$

$9 = 3 \times \underline{}$

$21 = 3 \times \underline{}$

The Four Times Table

Read the four times table. Then close the book
and write it out – how much can you remember?

1 x 4 = 4	5 x 4 = 20	9 x 4 = 36
2 x 4 = 8	6 x 4 = 24	10 x 4 = 40
3 x 4 = 12	7 x 4 = 28	11 x 4 = 44
4 x 4 = 16	8 x 4 = 32	12 x 4 = 48

Practise the four times table until you know it, then move on to the activities. You can use the cards in the middle of the book as flash cards and to play Matches and Dominoes too!

Fill in the answers below. Make sure you cover up the answers above first.

___ x 4 = 16   12 x ___ =48   ___ = 8 x 4

4 x ___ = 8   9 x 4 = ___   4 x ___ = 24

11 x 4 = ___   ___ x 4 = 12   4 x 5 = ___

___ = 1 x 4   ___ = 4 x 10   ___ x 4 = 28

Patterns

All the answers in the four times table end in 4, 8, 2, 6, 0 (the same numbers as the two times table, but they come in a different order).

1 x 4 = 4   5 x 4 = 20   9 x 4 = 36
2 x 4 = 8   6 x 4 = 24   10 x 4 = 40
3 x 4 = 12   7 x 4 = 28   11 x 4 = 44
4 x 4 = 16   8 x 4 = 32   12 x 4 = 48

Hopscotch

This hopscotch court has answers from the two times table in it. Colour in any that also appear in the four times table. What do you notice?

★★★
STAR TIP!
If you multiply a number by four, you can say you are quadrupling it.
★★★

2 4 6 8 10 12 14 16 18 20 22 24

24	58	9	2	18	12	11	36	91	48
49	8	34	10	3	48	50	2	24	69
9	6	36	25	46	32	35	16	53	9
69	2	23	12	4	24	40	30	11	49
4	16	44	28	16	40	24	8	36	16
7	50	19	36	12	28	48	1	10	14
17	71	59	40	8	20	16	10	14	3
54	6	8	25	24	3	5	24	26	24
5	12	17	58	16	10	25	61	36	17
48	18	7	1	4	9	47	7	9	44

Mystery Picture

Colour in all the spaces that have answers in the four times table. What picture do you get?

Maths Machine

This machine multiplies any number put into it by 4. Fill in the missing numbers.

10	→		→	
3	→		→	
	→	×4	→	20
8	→		→	
6	→		→	

Planet Hop

Draw a safe path for the rocket. It can only travel to planets that are answers in the four times table.

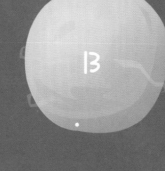 13

29  43

33

 45

 16

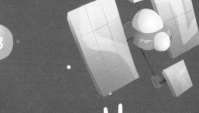 Home

24

 8

 40

36

18

Red Leader

Circle the rockets that belong with Squadron Leader 12. If they belong, their sums have the answer 12.

 12 x 1

5 x 5

4 x 8

3 x 4

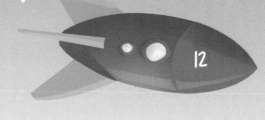 12

2 x 10

10 x 5

6 x 2

4 x 3

23

The Eight Times Table

Read the eight times table. Then close the book
and write it out – how much can you remember?

1 x 8 = 8	5 x 8 = 40	9 x 8 = 72
2 x 8 = 16	6 x 8 = 48	10 x 8 = 80
3 x 8 = 24	7 x 8 = 56	11 x 8 = 88
4 x 8 = 32	8 x 8 = 64	12 x 8 = 96

Practise the eight times table until you know it. Then use the
cards in the middle of the book as flash cards and to play Matches
and Dominoes as well!

**Fill in the answers below. Make sure you cover up the
answers above first.**

___ x 8 = 72   12 x ___ = 96   ___ = 8 x 8

3 x ___ = 24   4 x 8 = ___   7 x ___ = 56

11 x 8 = ___   ___ x 8 = 48   8 x 2 = ___

___ = 1 x 8   ___ = 8 x 10   ___ x 8 = 40

Patterns

All the answers in the eight times table end in
8, 6, 4, 2, 0…(that's counting down in twos).

$1 \times 8 = 8$ $5 \times 8 = 40$ $9 \times 8 = 72$

$2 \times 8 = 16$ $6 \times 8 = 48$ $10 \times 8 = 80$

$3 \times 8 = 24$ $7 \times 8 = 56$ $11 \times 8 = 88$

$4 \times 8 = 32$ $8 \times 8 = 64$ $12 \times 8 = 96$

Number Square Colouring

1	2	3	4	5	6	7	8	9	10
11	12	13	14	15	16	17	18	19	20
21	22	23	24	25	26	27	28	29	30
31	32	33	34	35	36	37	38	39	40
41	42	43	44	45	46	47	48	49	50
51	52	53	54	55	56	57	58	59	60
61	62	63	64	65	66	67	68	69	70
71	72	73	74	75	76	77	78	79	80
81	82	83	84	85	86	87	88	89	90
91	92	93	94	95	96	97	98	99	100

Colour all the numbers that are answers in the eight times table.

Now add to this picture by circling all the numbers that are answers in the four times table in a different colour.

STAR TIP!
All the numbers in the eight times table are exactly double those in the four times table.

Planet Hop

Draw a safe path for the rocket. It can only travel to planets that are answers in the eight times table.

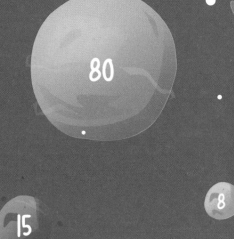

80

63

25

91

15

8

Home

48

6

64

38

55

Maths Machine

This machine multiplies any number put into it by 8. Fill in the missing numbers.

	×8	
	→	16
7	→	
	→	80
5	→	
8	→	

26

Red Leader

Circle the rockets that belong with Squadron Leader 40.
If they belong, their calculations have the answer 40.

Mystery Picture

Colour in all the spaces that have answers in the eight times table. What picture do you get?

The Answers

The Two Times Table

Page 6
Mystery Picture
The picture is an alien!

Maths Machine
The missing numbers are: 4, 3, 14, 18 and 11.

Page 7
Planet Hop
The rocket should hop to 8, 16, 22 and 2 to get home.

Crack the Door Code!
The code is: 12, 3, 4, 5.

The Ten Times Table

Page 9
Mystery Picture
The picture is a rocket and a planet.

Page 10
Through the Stars
The route is: 120, 60, 100, 40, 80, 10, 90, 30, 20 and 70.

Maths Machine
The missing numbers are: 10, 60, 5, 90 and 110.

Page 11
Crack the Door Code!
The code is: 8, 2, 9, 1.

Pick Your Spaceship Crew
There are five crew members: 20, 110, 90, 60 and 30.

The Five Times Table

Page 13
Hopscotch
All the answers that are in the ten times table appear on every other square, because every other answer in the five times table is also in the ten times table.

Page 14
Crack the Door Code!
The code is: 3, 6, 12, 9.

Secret Message
The message is "HI".

Page 15
Red Leader
The rockets that belong with Squadron Leader 20 are: 2 x 10, 4 x 5 and 10 x 2.

Through the Stars
The route is: 15, 50, 45, 5, 35, 25, 30 and 55.

The Three Times Table

Page 18
Maths Machine
The missing numbers are: 27, 4, 6, 7 and 36.

Mystery Picture
The picture is a star!

Page 19
Pick Your Spaceship Crew
There are five crew members: 12, 24, 18, 30 and 21.

Crack the Door Code!
The code is: 12, 10, 3, 7.

The Four Times Table

Page 21
Hopscotch
All the answers that are in the four times table appear on every other square, because every other answer in the two times table is also in the four times table.

Page 22
Mystery Picture
The picture is the Sun.

Maths Machine
The missing numbers are: 40, 12, 5, 32 and 24.

Page 23
Planet Hop
The rocket should hop to 36, 8, 16, 24 and 40 to get home.

Red Leader
The rockets that belong with Squadron Leader 12 are: 3 x 4, 6 x 2, 4 x 3 and 12 x 1.

The Eight Times Table

Page 26
Planet Hop
The rocket should hop to 64, 48, 80 and 8 to get home.

Maths Machine
The missing numbers are: 2, 56, 10, 40 and 64.

Page 27
Red Leader
The rockets that belong with Squadron Leader 40 are 5 x 8, 4 x 10, 8 x 5 and 10 x 4.

Mystery Picture
The picture is an astronaut!

Use Your Game Cards To...

1. Practise with Flash Cards

It's easy to practise any table using these cards. Each card has:

A Matches side:

A Domino side:

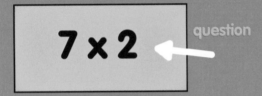

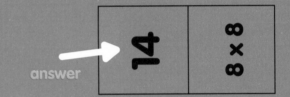

The Domino side has a number on it. This is the answer to the sum on the Matches side. The Domino side also has another sum.

- Carefully tear out the cards for the table you need.
- Put them all sum (Matches) side up and shuffle them.
- See if you can remember the answer to each sum.
- Turn the card over to check the answer – it appears on the Domino side.
- When you remember the table well, see how fast you can go!

2. Play Matches

Matches is a fun and simple way to practise tables. You will need:
- 2-4 players.
- To be able to do calculations in at least three tables.

How to Play:
- Select the cards for the tables you know or are learning now.
- Shuffle and divide the cards between the players.

- Everybody should hold their cards so that other players can't see them.
- Each player in turn puts a card down in the middle, Matches side up.
- A 'match' happens when you can see more than one sum that has the same answer. For example:

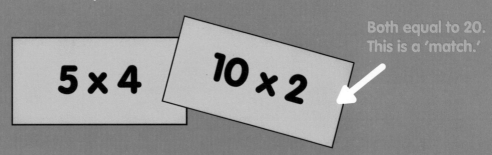

Both equal to 20. This is a 'match.'

- If there is a 'match', the first player to shout "match" wins all the cards in the middle. If someone shouts "match" incorrectly, they have to put a card in the middle.
- The first person to get all the cards is the winner!

3. Play Dominoes

To play times table Dominoes, you will need:
- 2-4 players.
- To know at least the two, ten and five times tables. (You can also add in the three, four and eight times tables if you know them or are learning them now.)

How to Play:

- Sort out the cards you need, shuffle them and put them all Domino side down.
- Deal all the cards out to the players and ask them to look at the Domino side.
- If you are using the two, ten and five times tables only, the player with a 10 starts. (If you are also using the cards from the three, four and eight times tables, then the player with a 20 starts.)
- The player with the 10 (or 20) puts it on the table, Domino side up.
- If the next player has a card that matches, he or she can put it next to this first Domino.

A card matches if...
The sums match:

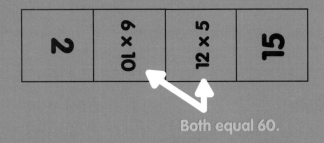

Both equal 60.

Or if the sum matches a number:

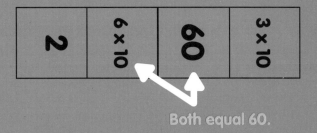

Both equal 60.

You can place the cards in any direction.

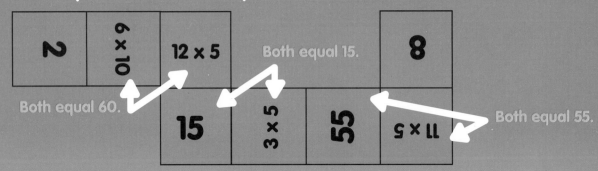

Both equal 15.

Both equal 60.

Both equal 55.

If the player cannot go, he or she misses a turn. The first player to use their last domino is the winner!

4. To Find Your Alien Name

To find your alien name, you need the 24 cards that have names, and the domino cards for the times tables you know or are learning. You can play this game with any (or all!) of the tables.

How to Play:

- Pick a Domino card and look at the number.
- Think about the tables sums you know which have that number as an answer. For example, if you pick the domino card that reads '90', you can work out that 90 = 9 x 10.
- Then pick the alien name cards with the numbers you have chosen on them and put them together to make your alien name. For example if you pick '9' (Konk) and '10' (Blurg) your alien name would be Konk Blurg.
- Try it with lots of numbers and see what name you get!